The Littlest Christmas Tree

Printed in the United States of America

ISBN 979-8-89114-244-2 (sc)
ISBN 979-8-89114-245-9 (e)

Library of Congress Control Number: 2025923222

2025.12.08

MainSpring Books
5901 W. Century Blvd
Suite 750
Los Angeles, CA, US, 90045

www.mainspringbooks.com

The Littlest Christmas Tree

Kathleen Whitham

In the expansive Christmas tree lot adjacent to the supermarket, next to all the tall Frazer firs, elegant white spruces, and bushy Scotch pines, as if pushed aside, the littlest tree waited.

She was so excited about the opportunity to brighten up someone's home, to hear the laughter of the children as they help hang bulbs and balls and candy canes, to watch their faces light up upon seeing her own lights twinkling, casting brilliant reflections off the shining ornaments, to see their smiles on Christmas morning as they discover the presents wrapped in colorful paper beneath her branches.

Maybe she'd even catch a glimpse of Santa Claus tiptoeing across the room to deliver toys for her family and hear the reindeer prancing and pawing on the roof as they wait for Santa to rise back up the chimney.

The littlest tree kept waiting. One by one, the larger trees in the lot were selected, paid for, taken down, and loaded on top of cars and into pickup trucks for delivery.

I know my turn will come soon, she thought to herself again and again. She waited and waited as the other trees departed to go adorn the homes, apartments, businesses, and shop windows of the surrounding area. The lot appeared barren, almost empty.

It was Christmas Eve. Little tears, or were they snowflakes, formed on her needles and glowed in the late-afternoon sunlight. Then it was dusk. Night was coming. The moon rose in the sky, causing the little tree's icicle-covered branches to sparkle in the night. A light dusting of snow began to fall softly.

A bird came and nestled in her thick branches. Then a small gray squirrel scrambled up her trunk and settled down for the night. A fine mist of sleet began to swirl about. Soon a doe and her fawn burrowed in close to lie down beneath her lower branches, snuggling next to her tiny trunk to shield themselves from the cold, wind, and sleet

The littlest tree was reminded of the story of the humble stable housing the animals and protecting them from the cold and the dangers of that night long ago when our Savior came into the world.

The stars shone brightly in the silence of this Christmas Eve night, just as they had the night Jesus was born.

The littlest tree listened quietly to hear the winter wind whipping unobstructed across the tree lot, or maybe what she really heard was the angels singing the message of the Christ child's birth and joy, peace on earth, and goodwill among all people. And as she stood there, strong and steady in the stillness, shielding the little bird, the squirrel, and the mother and baby deer, she felt happy and at peace. This was where she belonged, what she was meant to do, and what's more, she could even hear the angels singing in the heavens.

Remember, you don't have to be big to do big things. Do what God created you to do. Be kind, help those in need, and listen quietly and carefully in the stillness. You too will be able to hear the angels sing, to learn what you have been chosen to do, and to discover the true meaning of Christmas.

PEACE ON EARTH
GOOD WILL AMONG ALL

About the Author

Kathleen, a graduate of Indiana University with a master's degree from the University of North Carolina, is a French teacher with over forty years of experience. She is also the owner and chief chef of a pie-making business in Hillsborough, North Carolina. However, she considers her role as mother of five sons and grandmother of eight to be the role of utmost importance in her life. She has written a number of stories for the grandchildren. As a matter of fact, *The Littlest Christmas Tree* was born as a story she wrote for her grandchildren (when there were only five of them) a few years ago.